This story is inspired by the first flight of living creatures in an aircraft. On September 19, 1783, the Montgolfier brothers demonstrated their new invention, the hot-air balloon, or *montgolfière*, at the Palace of Versailles. Louis XVI, the king of France, and his queen, Marie Antoinette, were in attendance. Considered too dangerous for human passengers, the balloon carried a sheep, a duck, and a hen in its basket. It flew for about eight minutes, covered a distance of roughly two miles, and reached an altitude of about fifteen hundred feet before landing safely. The animals' ride caused a sensation, and the first human flight followed a few months later. By the end of 1783, Louis XVI had ennobled the Montgolfier family in recognition of the brothers' achievement, which perhaps led to a royal celebration like the one depicted here. While the role of talking animals in the storming of the Bastille in 1789 can't be confirmed with factual evidence, the advances in aeronautics that took place right around the time of the French Revolution are a stirring part of history.

A King Seen
from the Sky

Bruno Gibert

The J. Paul Getty Museum
Los Angeles

September 19, 1783, is a great day for the royal court at the Palace of Versailles. In the gardens, everyone waits for the king of France.

Voilà! Here he is.

His Majesty is going to watch the first flight of a hot-air balloon.
This one was made by the Montgolfier brothers.

Three courageous beasts—
a duck,
a sheep,
and a hen—climb aboard the flimsy contraption.

Filled with hot air, the balloon lifts slowly into the sky.

The weather is fair,
the wind is gentle,
and the animals are delighted.
They experience something no one else has before:

the earth seen from the sky.

From way up high, the elegant palace
looks like three huge shoeboxes!

And the crowd is just a handful of gravel
tossed on the ground.

The lovely garden
resembles a card game.
"It also makes me think of a clown
with a runny nose!" says the sheep,
pointing to the fountain far below.

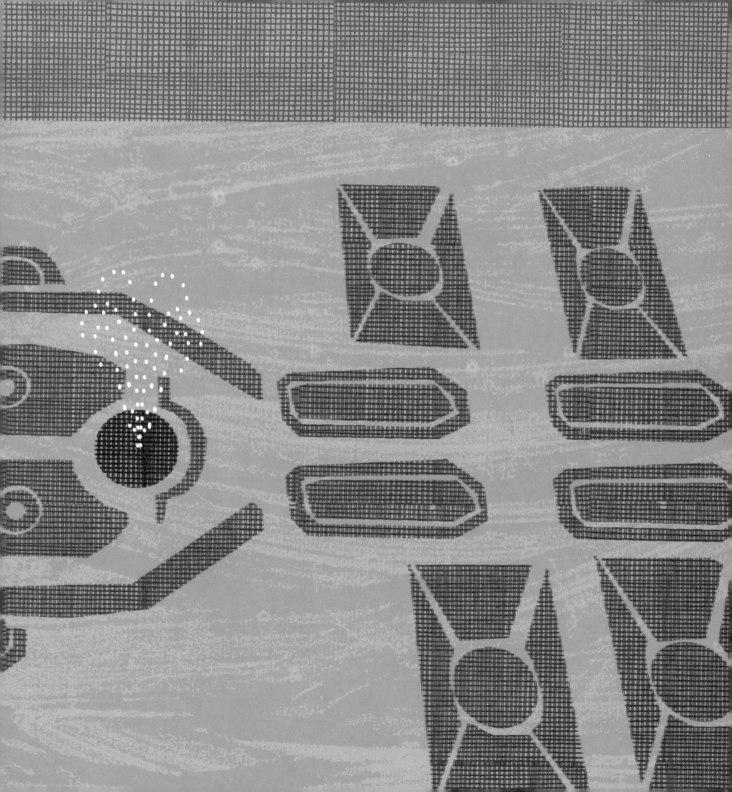

The balloon rises higher.
The countryside around the palace
transforms into a plate of spinach
mashed with a fork.

"And look at all those ants!"
cries the duck, looking at the farmers
working in a field no larger
than a handkerchief.

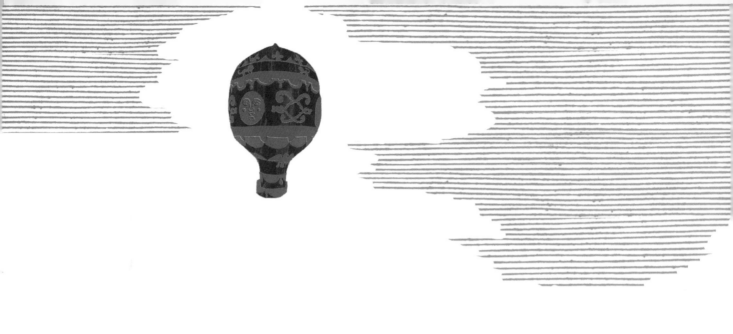

The balloon gently descends
until once again it rests on solid ground.

The animals, safe and sound, are given a hero's welcome.
And they deserve it: after all, these three farm animals are
the world's first air travelers!

During the banquet held in their honor,
they tell the king what they saw:
shoeboxes, a handful of gravel, a clown with a cold,
a plate of spinach, and some ants.

The king, who is vain,
like all kings are,
asks them, "And I?
From the greatest heights,
what did I look like?"

The animals reply together,
"Oh, Sire, you looked no larger
than the nose of a rat—or even smaller,
the eye of a mouse. Or maybe you were
the size of a tiny snail!"

Furious, the king immediately sends
the animals to jail at the Bastille!

Oh how poorly their bravery and honesty are rewarded!

The story could have ended there.

But on July 14, 1789—bang!
It's the Revolution!
The citizens of Paris, with rifles
and cannons, storm the Bastille!

Freed from jail, the animals are heroes once more.
From that day forward, they wear the red, white, and blue
cockade and carry the flag of the Revolution.

Then they decide to build the largest
flying machine ever seen, a kind
of enormous watermelon made
from canvas and wood.

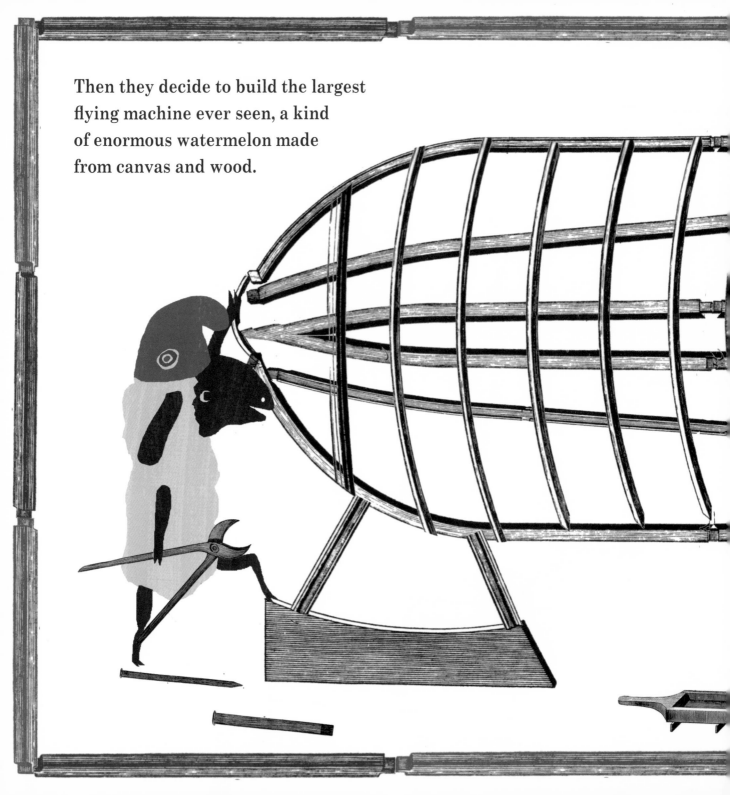

In their new airship,
the animals float peacefully into the sky.
It is summer, the air is calm, and everyone
is happy.

From way up above, the city
of Paris looks like a little village,
decorated for a celebration.
Fireworks whistle and boom.

It's Independence Day in France!

English edition © 2015 J. Paul Getty Trust

First published in the United States of America in 2015
by the J. Paul Getty Museum, Los Angeles

Getty Publications
1200 Getty Center Drive, Suite 500
Los Angeles, California 90049-1682
www.getty.edu/publications

Nola Butler, Ruth Evans Lane, and Elizabeth Nicholson, *Manuscript Editors*
Catherine Lorenz, *Designer*
Elizabeth Kahn, *Production Coordinator*

Distributed in the United States and Canada by the University of Chicago Press
Distributed outside the United States and Canada by Yale University Press, London

Printed and bound by Tien Wah Press, Malaysia (W60911)

Library of Congress Cataloging-in-Publication Data

Gibert, Bruno, 1961- author, illustrator.
  [Roi vu du ciel. English]
 A king seen from the sky / Bruno Gibert.
      pages cm
 Translation of: Roi vu du ciel / Bruno Gibert. Paris : Le Baron Perche, 2013.
 Summary: "In 1783, King Louis XVI and Queen Marie Antoinette of France watch a sheep,
a duck, and a hen take the first hot-air balloon ride"—Provided by publisher.
 ISBN 978-1-60606-460-3 (hardcover)
 1. Louis XVI, King of France, 1754–1793—Juvenile fiction. [1. Louis XVI, King of France,
1754–1793—Fiction. 2. Hot air balloons—Fiction. 3. Animals—Fiction. 4. Humorous stories.]
I. J. Paul Getty Museum, issuing body. II. Title.
 PZ7.G339253Kl 2015
 [E]—dc23
                    2015018128

Text and illustrations by Bruno Gibert
Translated from the French by Andrew Goodhouse

Originally published as *Un roi vu du ciel* © 2013 Éditions Le Baron Perché, Paris

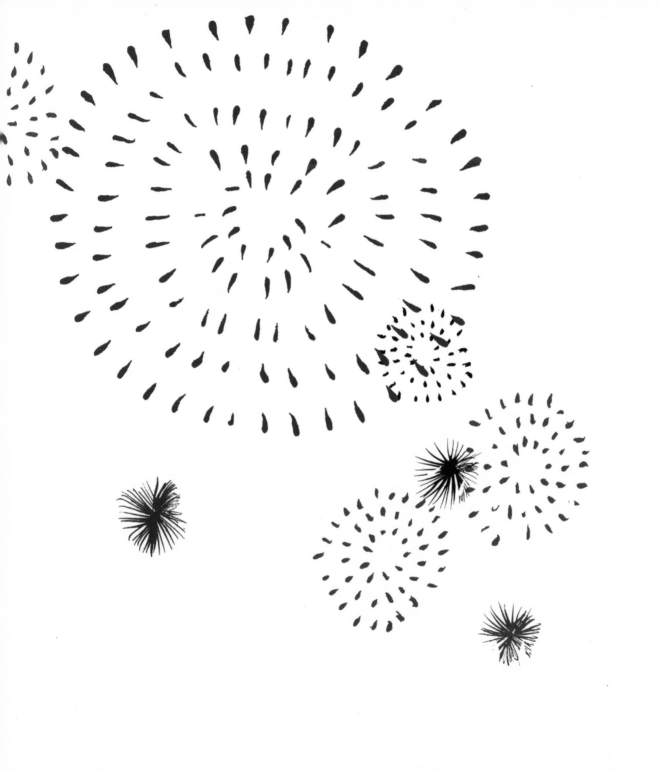